This book belongs to...

Daisy Finds Her Smile

First published in 2021 by

Panocub, an imprint of Panoma Press Ltd
48 St Vincent Drive, St Albans, Herts, AL1 5SJ, UK

info@panocub.com
www.panocub.com

info@panomapress.com
www.panomapress.com

Book illustrations by Sarah Alicia Smith
Book layout by Neil Coe

978-1-838144-62-3

The right of Melanie Broughton to be identified as the author of this work has been asserted in accordance with sections 77 and 78 of the Copyright, Designs and Patents Act 1988.

A CIP catalogue record for this book is available from the British Library.

All rights reserved. No part of this book may be reproduced in any material form (including photocopying or storing in any medium by electronic means and whether or not transiently or incidentally to some other use of this publication) without the written permission of the copyright holder except in accordance with the provisions of the Copyright, Designs and Patents Act 1988. Applications for the copyright holder's written permission to reproduce any part of this publication should be addressed to the publishers.

This book is available online and in bookstores.

Copyright 2021 Melanie Broughton

Dedication

This book is dedicated to my children Shamus, Alice and Archie, who heard me talk about writing Daisy's story for 12 years – I got there in the end. Don't ever give up on your dreams.

A huge thank you to my friend Fiona Unwin, who has helped bring the story of Daisy to life.

To anyone of any age who has suffered at the hands of bullies, I hope the message in this book touches your heart and gives you strength. Remember, each and every one of you is loved and very special, just as you are.

Daisy was a little duck

Who started life without much luck.

Upon her head she wore a bonnet,

With soft and fluffy feathers on it.

Quack, Quack, Quack.

As a duckling she banged her head
Which made it feel as heavy as lead.
Often when she waddled around
She would fall down to the ground.

Quack, Quack, Quack.

She lived with some chickens in a very big pen
But soon they saw she wasn't one of them.
So, sadly, as the days went by
They were cruel and mean – they made Daisy cry.

Quack, Quack, Quack.

Quack,

Quack,

Quack.

So, in the bushes she would hide away.

At times this would be for more than a day.

She braved coming out for a bite to eat

The chickens would chase her so she was forced to retreat.

Oh poor Daisy, so lonely and sad.

If she only had friends, things wouldn't feel so bad.

So she stayed in the bushes, right at the back.

Then one day, oh joy, she heard a faint quack.

Quack,

Quack,

Quack.

Was it really a quack and not just a cluck?

Could this be her lucky day? Was that really a duck?

Her owner, Mrs B, came into the pen

And, sure enough, Daisy heard the quack again.

Quack, Quack, Quack.

Mrs B knelt down and called Daisy's name
And begged poor Daisy to come out again.
"Be brave, little duck," she said. "See who is here!"
So Daisy crept out and saw two ducks, clear as clear.

Quack, Quack, Quack.

She stood, she stared, she couldn't believe her luck.
What a wonderful day: they really were ducks.
"Look," said Mrs B, "you have some friends to make.
Let me introduce you to Digby and Drake."

Quack,
Quack,
Quack.

Daisy felt brave with Digby and Drake.

They dreamed that, one day, they could swim on a lake.

But, for now, they were happy in their big pen,

Ready to stand up to the chickens now and again.

"Follow me," Daisy said. "Take a look around.
This is your home, where you can feel safe and sound.
I will protect you from the chickens who are bad
And if any of them hurt you, I will be mad."

Quack,

Quack,

Quack.

But the chickens didn't hurt them, they didn't seem to care.

Nor did they stand up tall and give Daisy their horrid stare.

The trio were happy as they waddled around

And Digby and Drake helped Daisy when she fell to the ground.

Quack,
Quack,
Quack.

They quacked, they flapped and they splashed every day.
What fun they had as they whiled the time away!
Having friends in your life is just the best feeling,
You feel happy and loved, it really is healing.

Quack, Quack, Quack.

You see, when the world seems a lonely place,
You just need your friends to bring a smile to your face.
Then you can stand up to anyone, however big or small.
Hold your head up high and stand up really tall.

Quack,

Quack,

Quack.

With love in your heart and a friend by your side,
You can journey through life with laughter and pride.
You can laugh, you can hug, you can love all the while
And the best thing of all is to have a big smile.

Quack,
Quack,
Quack.

For when you smile, your face lights up bright

And sometimes a smile makes your eyes shut tight.

Go on, try it – smile your best smile.

I bet it's the happiest in the world by a mile.

Quack,

Quack,

Quack.

So be like Daisy, Digby and Drake.

Just try your best smile, see the difference it makes.

Look at someone, look right in their eyes,

Give them a smile and their heart will reach the skies.

I bet they're smiling back at you!

Quack, Quack, Quack.

Daisy Finds Her Smile – the story behind the story

This is a true story of Daisy, a crested duck I purchased from a livestock market in 2008. She was a very cheerful little duck and did a lot of quacking. However, I noticed she had some sort of disability, as she fell over frequently, especially when she flapped her wings or walked too fast. She would plant her beak in the ground and waggle her feet in order to right herself.

I fenced off part of my chicken pen for Daisy as I thought it would be fun to tame her.

After a while, I let her out into the big pen with the chickens. A few days later, there was no more quacking from Daisy. The chickens had been horrid to her and poor Daisy was hiding in the bushes. Gandalf the cockerel was especially beastly to her. He would repeatedly chase her and peck at her. He encouraged the other chickens to do the same and they seemed to take pleasure in tormenting her.

I was so upset for Daisy that I went back to the market and bought two more ducks, both of whom were crested Indian Runners and far taller than Daisy. Daisy's confidence grew almost immediately and she became the 'hostess', showing Digby and Drake around.

From then onwards, the chickens pretty much ignored her apart from the odd spat, but Daisy was bolder and happier with her friends by her side.

The ducks had a 'pond' (the bottom of a 45 gallon drum), which they loved to splash around in. Whilst one of them was in the pond, the others would run around it, quacking with excitement. It was wonderful to see them all so happy.

Parents' and Teachers' message

This book emphasises the importance of being kind, the joy of a smile and understanding that not all disabilities are visible.

I have put "Quack, Quack, Quack" between verses so the children can have a chorus to make the story more interactive. Perhaps they could 'flap' their wings.

Suggested questions and topics to cover with children to open up a discussion about bullying:

1. Do you all remember how sad Daisy was when the chickens were horrid and bullied her? How did that make her feel?

2. Ask the children to describe what they think bullying is.

    Teasing. Name calling. Hitting. Pushing. Not including someone.

    Making fun of others.

3. Daisy used to fall over when she flapped her wings or walked too fast, but there was no visible sign of a disability. This can help children be more understanding and realise that just because you can't see a disability it doesn't mean it doesn't exist. Emphasise kindness and tolerance and that each of us is different.

4. You could do an exercise of thinking of words that rhyme in the poem.

    Drake, B as in Mrs B (Nanny Mcphee), cry, head, pen, day.

5. There were four words in the story, that some children may not have heard before, such as:

    Bonnet, Retreat, Trio and Pride

6. To finish, "Can you all practise your best smile. Did you know you all have SSP – Special Smiling Powers? Guess what? I bet if you smile at someone, you really will see them smiling back at you. It's a bit like magic!"

About the author

Melanie Broughton is a single mum of three grown-up children and lives near Newmarket, Suffolk.

She is passionate about photography and is an Equine Touch and VHT practitioner, which is a gentle, hands-on therapy to encourage healing and relaxation in horses and humans.

Melanie leads an active life and enjoys swimming, cycling, riding and walking, as well as gardening and looking after her chickens.

Animals have always been an important part of her life, and as a child she was frequently rescuing injured creatures.

When one of her children was bullied at school, she realised Daisy's story could open up discussions with children about bullying and steer them towards a kinder, fairer and more inclusive world.

About the artist

Sarah Alicia Smith is a Yorkshire-based artist specialising in watercolour and digital illustration.

Before becoming an artist, Sarah was an art teacher in secondary schools where she taught GCSE and A-Level students.

She now works as a full time artist from her home studio based in Otley, West Yorkshire. Sarah has a young family and takes a lot of inspiration from the beautiful Yorkshire Dales and countryside around her hometown.

Sarah's interests include running, walking and being creative.

Endorsements

"Melanie visited our school to give a reading, and through her 'quacking' book highlighted the importance of being kind and standing up to bullying. I am pleased to say that the message from Daisy is a great one – kindness is key to a happy life."

Magoo Giles, Founder and Principal, Knightsbridge School, London

"It is a joy to see a book for children that shows how not to snipe and mock our differences, but to enjoy the friendships that can arise when a group of varied folk accept individual challenges and work together as friends."

James Colthurst MBBS; BSC; MFHom; MBA; FRCS(Ed), Independent Medical Practitioner

"Children soak up and absorb everything we share with them, and *Daisy Finds Her Smile* is an enchanting story with a message of friendship and kindness. It's a story which I know will initiate lots of conversation with little ones and allow us to emphasise the importance of being kind. The rhyming text and beautiful illustrations make this book the perfect bedtime read, and one which both adults and children will enjoy equally!"

Louenna Hood, Norland Nanny and Childcare Consultant, Creator of The Nanny In Your Pocket app